या देवी सर्वभूतेषु माँ रूपेण संस्थिता
या देवी सर्वभूतेषु शक्ति रूपेण संस्थिता
या देवी सर्वभूतेषु शांति रूपेण संस्थिता
नमस्तस्यै नमस्तस्यै नमस्तस्यै नमो नमः

The Goddess who is ever present as the universal mother,
The Goddess who is ever present as the embodiment of power,
The Goddess who is ever present as the symbol of peace,
To her I bow, to her I bow, to her I bow.

To my superwomen
Christine and Karen

anjana
publishing

May 2016

Edited By Mudita Chauhan Mubayi

L, Orient Crest,
76 Peak Road, The Peak, Hong Kong

ISBN: 978-988-12395-9-4

Designed by Jump Web Services Ltd
Printed in Guangdong Province China
This book is printed on paper made from well-managed sustainable forest sources.

Amma, Tell Me About

Durga Puja!

Illustrated by Maulshree Somani

Written by Bhakti Mathur

The city is buzzing with excitement
There is hustle and bustle everywhere.
It is time for Durga Puja, the festival
Of song and dance, worship and prayer!

Malls teem with shoppers, buying new clothes,
To wear and to gift during the festive days.
The neighbourhood halls, too, are busy as ever,
As performers rehearse their musicals and play

Idols of Ma Durga get their finishing touches,
Still under cover, waiting to be unfurled.
Colourful *pandaals* have come up everywhere
To host the biggest outdoor festival in the world!

Ten days of worship to the divine Goddess,
The mother who nurtures us all in birth,
The loving daughter in whom we delight,
The guardian shielding us from evil on earth.

First is *Mahalaya*, when we invoke the Goddess,
Homes resound with songs and hymns at dawn.
Lovingly inviting Ma Durga to descend to earth,
"Wake up" - "*Jaago tumi jaago*", they sing on and on.

Shashti then arrives, day one of celebrations,
When Ma Durga leaves Shiva, her heavenly spouse.
With her children Ganesha, Lakshmi, Saraswati, Kartik
She visits earth, as if visiting her parents' house.

This is the time to welcome her amidst us.
Unveil her idols with devotion and love,
To ritual chants and beats of *dhaak* drums,
"Welcome *O Devi*, from the heavens above!"

We go hopping from one *pandaal* to another,
Wonderfully decorated, their doors are open to all.
Beautiful structures made of clay, brick and glass,
Shaped like a temple, a camel and even a football!

Then comes *Shaptami*, and festivities intensify.
We worship Ma Durga as Mother Nature this day.
Dhaaki drummers go all out to thrill the crowds,
We throng the streets, dancing our cares away.

The all-important day of *Ashtami* follows next,
Pushpanjali is offered, roses sweeten the air.
People shower their adoration on Ma Durga,
Thousands of voices unite in fervent prayer.

The *aarti* that night is breathtaking, as though
The stars themselves have come down to earth.
Hundreds of lamps illuminate the *pandaals*
As every face, every heart glows with mirth.

Intoxicating *dhuno* aroma slowly drifts up
From *dhunuchi*, the earthen incense burners,
Which the dancers balance on their palms,
To the beat of *dhaak* drums, rising in fervour.

Then comes *Nabami*, a day of feasting on delicacies,
Bhog is first offered to Ma, then to everyone else.
The menu is delicious: *khichudi*, *beguni*, *rosogullas*,
And yummy *sondesh* that in our mouths just melts!

The last day of Puja, *Bijoya Dashami* arrives,
In throngs married women play *sindoor khela*.
Smearing vermilion, on Ma Durga and each other,
Of femininity and friendship, it's a happy *mela*.

is the day of *Shubho Bijoya* or auspicious victory,

a Durga is remembered as the all-powerful one today.

e celebrate how good triumphed over evil,

r Ma defeated the demon Mahisha this day.

And then it is time to bid Ma Durga farewell,
She is taken in a grand procession to the sea.
Gently immersed in the waters she returns
To the mountains, to Shiva and her family.

"*Aashche bochor abar hobe!*" the words echo in the air,
As people exclaim enthusiastically, in good cheer.
We know that this will happen yet again and again...
For Ma Durga will visit us the same time next year!

Friends do *Kolakuli*, rubbing shoulders in ritual embrace,
"*Shubho Bijoya!*" "*Shubho Bijoya!*" they each other greet.
Wearing new clothes, we visit family, and with respect
Seek the blessings of our elders by touching their feet.

Then, suddenly, the festivities were over,
The last few days, so quickly had passed.
But, Klaka and Kiki had unfinished busines
"Amma, tell us about Durga!", they asked.

They all settled down and Amma started,
"This is the story of how Durga came to be
It starts with this creature most strange,
Who had heaven and earth at his mercy.

Once there was a demon named Mahisha,
Half-man, half-buffalo with enormous horns.
His body tough as steel, his tail like a whip,
He could change his shape into many forms.

But he was not happy, he had a burning desire,
He wanted the whole world to bow to him,
To accept him as supreme lord and master,
To fawn over him and fulfil his every whim.

So one fine day, he climbed a tall mountain,
Stood rock-like for years, deep in meditation.
Bearing the freezing cold and the blazing heat,
Praying to Brahma, the god of all creation.

Brahma finally appeared before the demon,
And said, "Mahisha, I am pleased with you!
Ask for anything you wish and it will be your
I promise to make your dream come true."

Losing not a moment, Mahisha exclaimed,
"I don't want to die, Lord, let me live forever!"
"Impossible! How can this be?" said Brahma,
"For life and death must always go together."

Crafty Mahisha thought for a moment and said,
"Grant that no god, no beast, no man can kill me!"
For that will make me powerful and invincible,
He thought, as he stomped his hooves in glee.

Brahma smiled and said, "Your wish is granted!
I hope you will use your newfound powers well."
Mahisha, of course, had no such intentions,
He declared war, transforming earth into hell.

Unconquerable himself, he conquered the world
And then he turned on the Gods in heaven.
"Submit before me now or prepare for battle,
High time you learnt to bow to a demon!"

"A demon or a donkey?" the Gods mocked him,
Laughing and sneering, they dismissed his threat.
Red with rage, shaking, Mahisha screamed,
"I will teach you a lesson you will not forget!"

He gathered an army of demons,
Like no one had ever seen before.
The earth shuddered beneath them,
As they marched off, ready for war.

The Gods too were ready, a battle broke out,
Swords clashed and arrows darkened the skies.
The deities pushed hard against Mahisha, but
Could not overcome him, much as they tried.

They realised that there was no easy way
To defeat the demon army and end the strife.
Their strength came to nought against Mahisha,
As long as Brahma's boon protected his life.

A divine meeting was then urgently called,
For the gods needed to form a new plan.
"To face Mahisha," said Vishnu, "We need
One who is not god, not beast, not man!"

Shiva and Brahma nodded in their approval,
They understood at once what Vishnu meant.
The all-powerful trio then came together,
To join their energies in single-minded intent.

From Brahma's brow emerged a bright flame,
Shiva's third eye emitted a dazzling light.
Vishnu radiated a ray of calm, blue energy,
Oh what an utterly mesmerising sight!

The triple powers upon coming together
Fused into a blaze, brighter than the sun.
And from it arose a wondrous, radiant being,
Not god, not beast, not man - but a woman!

Ten tough arms, eyes like hot embers,
Long tresses, as dark as the darkest night
Thus was created the magnificent Durga,
A super goddess unmatched in her might.

Shiva gave her his mighty trident,
The bow was a gift from the Wind God.
Vishnu presented her his golden discus,
The Fire God handed her an iron rod.

The Rain God offered his thunderbolt,
A quiver of arrows came from the Sun God.
And the rest of her armoury was this,
A mace, an axe, a shield and a sword.

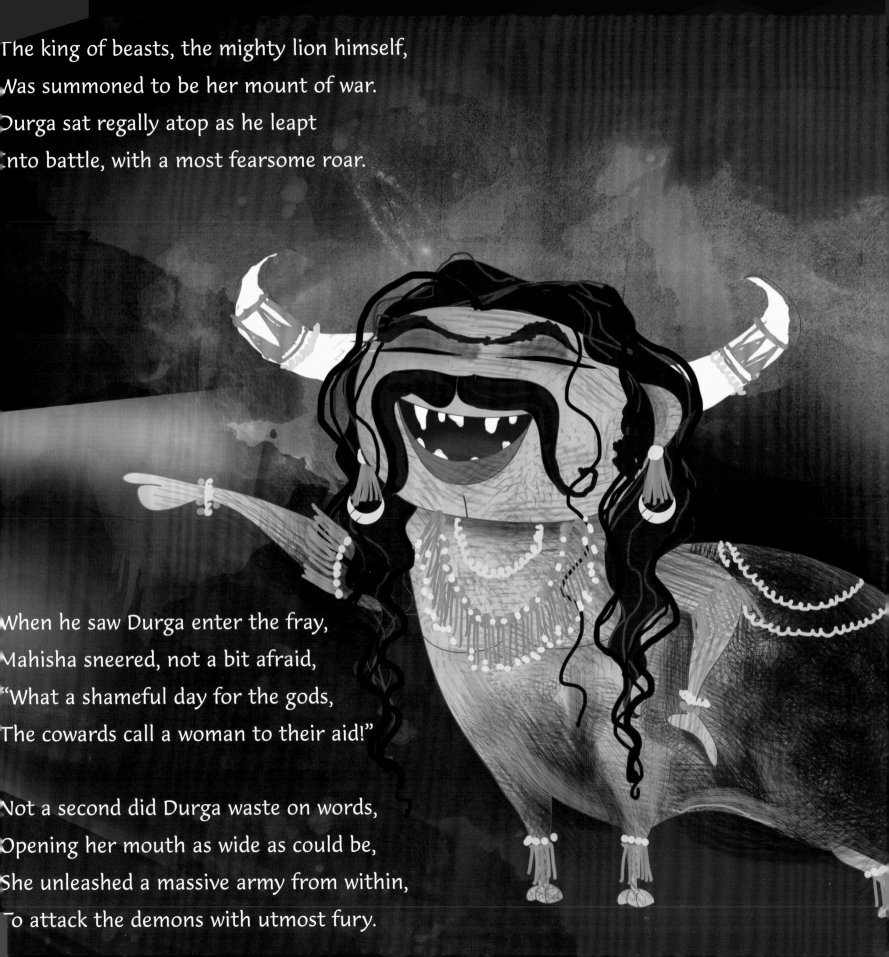

The king of beasts, the mighty lion himself,
Was summoned to be her mount of war.
Durga sat regally atop as he leapt
Into battle, with a most fearsome roar.

When he saw Durga enter the fray,
Mahisha sneered, not a bit afraid,
"What a shameful day for the gods,
The cowards call a woman to their aid!"

Not a second did Durga waste on words,
Opening her mouth as wide as could be,
She unleashed a massive army from within,
To attack the demons with utmost fury.

In one mighty leap, she came to face Mahisha,
A blow from her mace dashed him to the groun[d]
He magically transformed into a fierce lion
And with a dreadful roar prepared to bound.

Durga prepared to cut off the lion's head
But wily Mahisha pulled yet another trick.
Shape-shifting into a burly, beefy giant
He charged at Durga but she was quick.

She hurled a volley of arrows at the giant,
But he changed yet again, into an elephant.
Seizing Durga's lion with his long trunk,
Mahisha dragged them, looking triumphant.

Durga recovered, she cut off the elephant's trunk
With an almighty swish of her divine sword.
Lo and behold! Mahisha became a buffalo again,
Charging wildly at Durga, his energy restored.

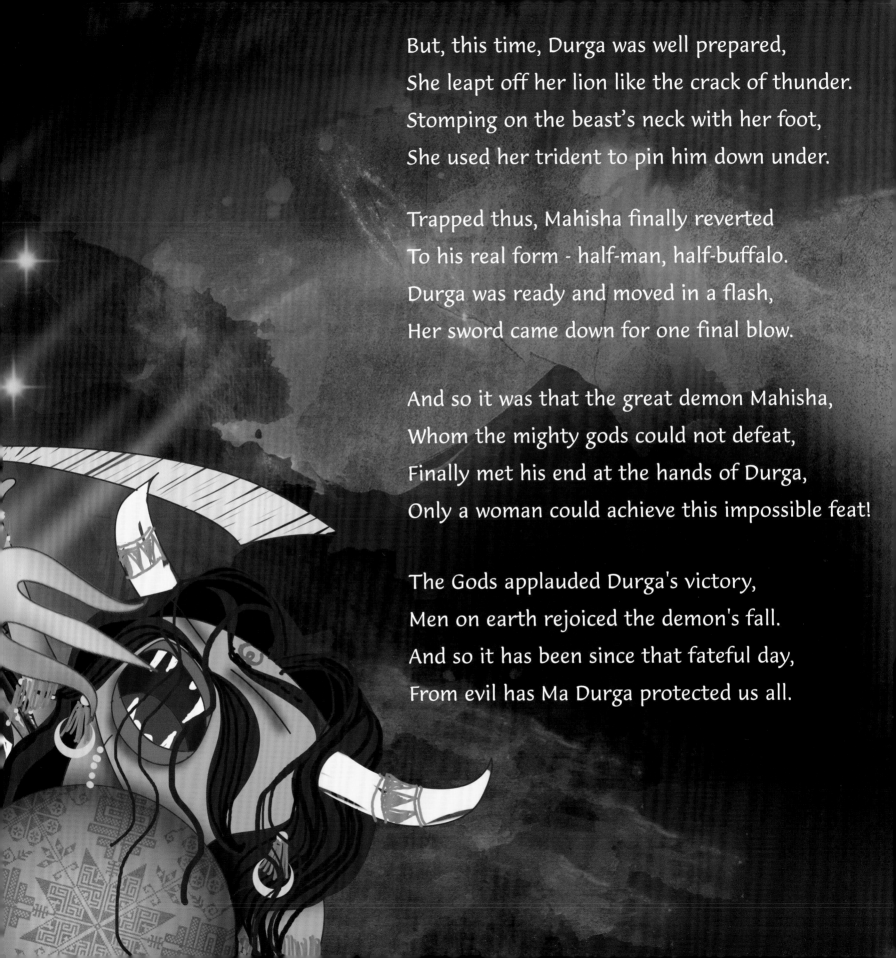

But, this time, Durga was well prepared,
She leapt off her lion like the crack of thunder.
Stomping on the beast's neck with her foot,
She used her trident to pin him down under.

Trapped thus, Mahisha finally reverted
To his real form - half-man, half-buffalo.
Durga was ready and moved in a flash,
Her sword came down for one final blow.

And so it was that the great demon Mahisha,
Whom the mighty gods could not defeat,
Finally met his end at the hands of Durga,
Only a woman could achieve this impossible feat!

The Gods applauded Durga's victory,
Men on earth rejoiced the demon's fall.
And so it has been since that fateful day,
From evil has Ma Durga protected us all.

So that, dear boys, was the story of Ma Durga,
The perfect example of womanhood is she.
She fiercely protects her loved ones from danger,
Even if super gentle at other times she may be.

Mahisha's mistake was one that many make
Of thinking a woman is only gentle and fra
They forget that she is *Shakti* incarnate,
The power within her can never, ever fail!"

Glossary

Aarti: worship ritual in which lamps with wicks soaked in ghee (purified butter) or camphor are lit and offered to one or more deities

Aashche bochor abar hobe: next year it shall happen again

Ashtami: the second day of Durga Puja

Beguni: a snack popular in Eastern India. Made of sliced brinjal (eggplant), battered and fried in oil

Bhog: food offered to the gods

Bijoya Dashami: the last day of Durga Puja

Devi: goddess

Dhaak: a type of drum

Dhaakis: drummers

Dhuno: a smoking mixture of camphor, incense, tinder and coconut husk that is poured inside the Dhunuchi

Dhunuchi: wide brimmed incense burners, traditionally made of clay and used during Aarti or in ritualised dance worship

Durga: means 'unconquerable'. She is the principal form of the mother goddess in Hinduism. She is known by a variety of names - Amba, Jagadamba, Parvati, Shakti, Adishakti, Parashakti and Devi. She is also known as Mahishasuramardini, the annihilator of Mahishasura. She is pure energy or strength, referred to as 'Shakti'

Durga Puja: also known as Durgotsava, the most important festival of Bengal, celebrates Goddess Durga and refers to the auspicious days called Mahalaya, Shashti, Shaptami, Ashtami, Nabami and Bijoya Dashami

Jaago: wake up

Khichudi: a South Asian dish made with rice and lentils (dal)

Kolakuli: a tradition in Bengal where people embrace each other three times and rub shoulders to celebrate

Ma: mother

Mahalaya: the sacred day marking a week before Durga Puja to herald the arrival of the Goddess and invite her to descend on earth, by chanting mantras and singing devotional songs, also the day to remember departed souls in the family, with the ritual of tarpan (libations) of water and sesame seeds

Mela: a public event organised to celebrate a special occasion

Nabami: the third day of Durga Puja

Pandaal: a fabricated temporary structure set up for public gatherings for worship, weddings and other occasions

Puja: to worship or to pray

Pushpanjali: an offering of flowers to the gods

Rosogulla: a syrupy dessert of ball-shaped dumplings of chhena (cottage cheese) and semolina dough, cooked in light syrup made of sugar

Sandesh: a Bengali dessert made of milk and sugar

Shakti: in Hinduism, Shakti means power or empowerment. It is the ancient cosmic energy that represents the dynamic forces that are thought to move through the entire universe. Shakti is the personification of the divine feminine creative power

Shaptami: the first day of Durga Puja

Shashti: the day the idol of Ma Durga is unveiled. It falls a day before Shaptami

Shubho Bijoya: shubho means auspicious, bijoya means victory, shubho bijoya means 'the auspicious victory'

Sindoor: traditional red-orange cosmetic powder, usually worn by married women in India along the parting in their hair

Sindoor Khela: a ritual in which married women anoint each other with sindoor. Khela means 'play'